Tiger
Tales

Written by Ronne Randall
Illustrated by Jacqueline East

Louis and Lisa Lion were just learning to pounce, and their dad had told them to practise as much as they could. So they were prowling through the jungle, looking for prey to pounce upon.

"There's something orange and blue and fluttery," whispered Lisa. "Here I go…"

POUNCE!

As Lisa pounced on the butterfly, Louis spotted something green and jumpy. He crept up and got ready to...

POUNCE!

Just then, Lisa caught a glimpse of black and yellow
fuzz. "Perfect for pouncing," she thought.
"Ready, steady…"

POUNCE!

"OUCH!"

cried Lisa, rubbing
her nose with her paw.

"Maybe a bumblebee isn't such a good pouncing target! In fact, I think I've had enough pouncing practice for one day."

"Me too," said Louis. "Let's find something else to do."

But as the two little cubs bounded through the jungle, Louis suddenly saw a flash of orange and black in some bushes.

"A stripey snake!" he whispered. "It's too good to pass up!" So he crouched down and waited and waited for just the right moment, and then he...

POUNCED!

"OWWWOOWW!"

came a voice from the bush. "What's got my tail?"

The 'snake' turned out to be attached to a stripey little cub, just the same size as Louis and Lisa!

"Who are you?" they asked.

"I'm Timmy Tiger," said the little cub. "My mum and dad and I have just moved here from The Other Side of the Jungle. Who are you?"

"We're Louis and Lisa Lion," said Lisa. "Would you like to see what this side of the jungle looks like?"

Timmy said he would love to.

"That's our river," said Louis proudly. "It's really muddy, and fun to paddle in."

"It's very nice," said Timmy, "but it's kind of small. On The Other Side of the Jungle, there's a river that's as wide as fifty tall palm trees laid end to end!"

"Gosh!" said Louis and Lisa.

"And I can swim across that river – and back – without stopping once!" added Timmy.

"We can't even swim," said Lisa. "Will you show us how?"

"Err… maybe another time," said Timmy. "I'm just getting over the sniffles, and Mum said I shouldn't swim for a while."

A little farther along, Louis and Lisa saw Howard Hippo wallowing merrily in the mud.

"Hi, Howard!" they called. "This is our new friend, Timmy Tiger!"

Howard opened his mouth in a happy hippo grin. "Nice to meet you!" he bellowed.

"Nice to meet you, too," said Timmy, keeping his distance.

"You know," said Timmy, as the three cubs scampered on, "on The Other Side of the Jungle there's a hippo whose mouth is so big that Mum and Dad and I can all sit inside it!"

"Really?" gasped Louis and Lisa.

"Oh, yes," Timmy assured them. "It's cool and shady in there on hot, sunny days!"

Before Louis and Lisa had a chance to think about that, something dropped down from a branch, right in front of them. Timmy jumped back, but Louis and Lisa smiled and said, "Hi, Seymour! Meet our new friend, Timmy Tiger."

"Greetingsssss," hissed

Seymour Snake. "Ssso niccce to make your aquaintancccce!"

"Nice to meet you, too," said Timmy,
a little uncertainly.
"Well, sssso long," said Seymour,

as he slithered off.
"Sssssee you sssssoon I suppose!"

As Seymour disappeared down the path, Timmy said, "On The Other Side of the Jungle, there are snakes as thick as tree trunks. In fact, when I was a baby, one of those snakes swallowed me whole!"

"Oh, no!" cried Louis and Lisa.

"Yes," Timmy went on, "but my dad saved me by hitting the snake on the head so that he would spit me out!"

"Really?" said Louis and Lisa, their eyes growing wider and wider.

"Yes," said Timmy. "My dad's really, really strong, and really, really big. He's twice as big as an elephant, and he can carry six gorillas on his back! And my mum can do amazing things. She can stand on her front paws and juggle coconuts with her hind legs, and… and…"

"...and what?" asked a smiling, normal-sized tiger, on the path in front of them. Standing next to him – on all four legs – was another smiling tiger.

"...and, here they are," said Timmy, a little sheepishly. "Mum and Dad, these are my new friends, Louis and Lisa Lion."

"We're delighted to meet you," said Mr and Mrs Tiger.

"And as you can see," Mrs Tiger added, "we are very ordinary and normal tigers."

"But what about all those amazing things Timmy told us?" asked Louis. "What about The Other Side of the Jungle?"

"The Other Side of the Jungle is just like this side," said Mr Tiger.

"You mean the river isn't as wide as fifty tall palm trees laid end to end?" asked Lisa.

"And there isn't a hippo whose mouth is big enough to sit in, or a snake who swallowed Timmy when he was a baby?"

"No, indeed!" laughed Mrs Tiger.

Timmy looked embarrassed. "Well, they were good stories," he said.

"Yes," said Mrs Tiger, "but they were just stories." She turned to Louis and Lisa. "Timmy didn't have any friends to play with on The Other Side of the Jungle, so he spent all his time making up fantastic stories and imagining amazing adventures."

"But now that he's got friends like you two to play with," said Mr Tiger, "perhaps he'll have some real adventures, just as exciting as the ones in his stories!"

"And there are still more friends to meet, Timmy," Lisa said. "Wait till we introduce you to Mickey and Maxine Monkey, and Chico Chimp!"

"You know, there are monkeys and chimps on The Other Side of the Jungle, too," said Timmy.

"Really?" said Louis and Lisa, glancing at one another.

"Yes," said Timmy, "but actually, I didn't know them. I can't wait to meet Mickey and Maxine and Chico!"